Where Bread Comes From

Dear Ryla –
 Enjoy reading my
story. I hope someday
you will come visit me
at Shangri La Farm.
 Best wishes
 April Golden
 &KA
 Elaine Taylor
 10/14/2

April Golden

PAGE PUBLISHING, INC.
Conneaut Lake, PA

First originally published by Page Publishing 2020

ISBN 978-1-64584-805-9 (hc)
ISBN 978-1-64584-804-2 (digital)

Printed in the United States of America

The author recommends using organic and non-GMO ingredients. It is our responsibility to teach the children about organic and non-GMO foods so that they may make informed decisions for generations to come.

—From the Chronicles of the Army of Love. Peace. Etc. '19

A long time ago in a place called Shangri La Farm, there was a lady farmer who wanted to teach everyone she could about where bread came from. Farmer Elaine had some friends who taught in a charter school in Brooklyn, New York. They loved to bring their kindergarten classes to the farm to learn about where bread came from and to experience all the natural and wonderful aspects about farm life. Their journey was a long ride on a very big bus. They rode for nearly two hours, filled with excitement.

It was a lovely time of year when the class came to the farm. It was autumn when the trees had turned a lovely yellow, orange, and crimson color. There was a chill in the air, a little frost on the pumpkin, and a sliver of ice in the water bucket. If we were lucky, the sun would shine brightly to keep us warm.

Early in the morning on the day of their arrival, Farmer Elaine had many chores to do before the children would arrive. She wanted everyone to have a fun and interesting day.

As Farmer Elaine went out to feed the animals their breakfast, she happened to notice a small bird had fallen into a water bucket while trying to get a drink of water. The bird was still alive but very cold and shivering. Farmer Elaine quickly picked her up and gently put the fragile bird inside of her jacket, under her armpit, where it was very warm. She went back to caring for and feeding the animals, but she could only use one hand while she carefully nurtured the little bird.

Mrs. Love, Farmer Elaine's good friend, came to help with the program. When she arrived, she was given the little bird to carefully care for inside of her sweater.

It was time to set up the hall for when the children arrive. Little bags of wheat seeds were filled to hand out to each student to plant. The grain milling machine was set up for the children to experience the grinding of the wheat seeds into flour. The ingredients for making the bread—flour, yeast, oil, sugar, salt, and water—were placed at each table. There were fifty balls of premade dough for each student to mush around and knead, for them to take home and bake in their oven. The farm store oven was preheated. And everything was ready to go.

Yeah! The bus finally arrived. Farmer Elaine and Mrs. Love and the six little Jack Russell doggies greeted the children as they came off the bus. Everyone walked single file to the pond where they gathered.

Farmer Elaine welcomed everyone and talked to the class about what they would be doing while on the farm. "Today we are going to plant wheat seeds out in the big field." She showed them what the wheat would look like after it had grown for a few months.

Each child received a bag of wheat seeds. She explained that the wheat seeds were going to be planted and it would grow throughout the winter and spring and then be harvested next summer.

"We will walk in single file out to the big field where we will plant the seeds in a straight row and then gently cover them with little soil. Then everyone can sprinkle whatever seeds they have left all around the field. Along the way, we will stop at the hen house and take an egg out of the nest and gently place it into the basket that Mrs. Love is holding."

The class passed by the barnyard where they saw the horses, pigs, chickens, goods, goats, and barn cat. Everyone got the chance to walk through the greenhouse to feel the warmth of the sun giving life to the plants inside.

Soon they reached the beautifully tilled field where they would plant the seeds.

"Please, carefully put them on the ground, in the row, and cover them carefully with a little bit of soil."

After their work was done, everyone got a chance to run around freely and happily.

"Now we are going back to the barn center where we will have some lunch."

*****

"We will need to mill some seeds into flour then bake some bread. Let us mix our flour, water, yeast, salt, sugar, oil, and, an egg then mush it around until it becomes a ball of dough. We will put it in a bowl and set it into a warm place so that the yeast will come to life and the dough will rise, doubling in size. That will take about two hours."

The children got to take that home with them and bake it there.

Since Farmer Elaine had done her homework, there were loaves of bread already in the oven. The aroma of freshly baking bread smelled so good. The children could then see where bread came from as Farmer Elaine took the loaves out of the oven. Everyone enjoyed the delicious warm bread as it came out of the oven. So yummy.

The time had passed so quickly and now it was time to go home. Everyone gathered up their belongings and their bag of dough and got ready to get back on the bus.

Someone asked Mrs. Love how the little birdie was, and as she opened her sweater to check on her, she flew away.

Everyone was so happy. Farmer Elaine and Mrs. Love waved farewell and sent them all on their way.

About the Author

 The author loves storytelling. She has lived the most interesting and full life of anyone she has ever known. Her goal is to touch as many lives as she possibly can while she is alive and reach the hearts of everyone she meets by expressing the importance of loving one another deeply. She is dedicated to helping others and her community. She is a writer, inventor, entrepreneur, farmer, embroiderer, public servant, and all-around positive human being dedicated to the betterment of society by any means possible. She has complete faith in God and looks for that of God in each and everyone and everything. She has worked hard her whole life and continues to do so in her retirement, offering others the opportunity to find their path in life by experiencing a respite in her farm. All is good in her world.

CPSIA information can be obtained
at www.ICGtesting.com
Printed in the USA
BVHW092311080820
585858BV00002B/5